WIND-WILD DOG

Written by **Barbara Joosse** • Illustrated by **Kate Kiesler**

Henry Holt and Company • New York

Henry Holt and Company, LLC
Publishers since 1866
175 Fifth Avenue
New York, New York 10010
www.henryholtchildrensbooks.com

Distributed in Canada by H. B. Fenn and Company Ltd.

Library of Congress Cataloging-in-Publication Data
Joosse, Barbara M.
Wind-wild dog / by Barbara Joosse; illustrated by Kate Kiesler.—1st ed.
p.   cm.
Summary: Ziva, a "wind-wild" young sled dog, decides whether to stay with the man
who has trained her or to run free with the wolves and wind.
ISBN-13: 978-0-8050-7053-8 / ISBN-10: 0-8050-7053-2
[1. Sled dogs—Fiction. 2. Dogs—Fiction. 3. Alaska—Fiction.] I. Kiesler, Kate, ill. II. Title.
PZ7.J7435WI 2006   [E]—dc22   2005020055

First Edition—2006 / Designed by Laurent Linn
The illustrator used oils to create the illustrations for this book.
Printed in China on acid-free paper. ∞

1 3 5 7 9 10 8 6 4 2

For the wind-wild man, CT Whitehouse,
and his beloved dog, Ziva, who inspired this story
—B. J.

For Sophie, my wind-wild dog
—K. K.

The night Ziva was born, the wind held its breath.

Ziva's mother, a sled dog, licked her newborn pup, then nuzzled her softly. Ziva squirmed into the pile of pups and lapped and smacked at her mother's milk.

Suddenly the wind picked up.

Wolves prowled against the moon.

Ziva pointed her small, wet nose into the wind and sniffed.

Weeks later, Ziva opened her puppy eyes. One eye was brown, the other blue.

Two-color eyes spooked most mushers. They said it made a dog half-wild.

One by one, the mushers chose other pups, never Ziva.

Left alone, Ziva grew skittish. Sometimes when the moon came out and she heard wolves howl, Ziva dug at the dirt and threw her shoulders against the chain. She wanted to run.

One day a man stopped at Ziva's kennel.

He saw the wind-wild dog and took a liking to her.

The Man calculated the end of Ziva's chain and sat there with his back to her. Ziva stood square and barked. The Man didn't move. Ziva slunk forward, then grew shy and went back again. The Man waited.

Ziva sniffed the air around the Man. Then she sniffed his back. The Man offered her a biscuit. Ziva ate it, licking the crumbs from his hand.

The Man took Ziva home.

The pack yapped and howled when they smelled a new dog. Ziva crouched against the Man's leg, and he patted her.

That night Ziva thought she saw the shadow of a wolf running across the moon. She pricked up her ears to hear the howl, but it didn't come. The figure turned, came closer, closer still. It wasn't a wolf. It was the Man! He ran as if he were wild, too.

As Ziva curled up to sleep, she smelled the Man on her fur.

Weeks passed. Every morning, Ziva watched the Man come through the square of yellow.

He fed her first, then the rest of the pack.

The Man's food was regular, morning and night. His hand was gentle, never mean. Now when he came through the door, Ziva yapped until he set her free. Then she shadowed his boot steps. She wanted to be close.

At last Ziva was ready for training.

Slowly, gently, the Man put a harness on her. At first she flattened to the ground. But he talked to Ziva with a steady voice until she grew used to the harness.

Then the Man tied a log behind Ziva so she could feel the pull.
Ziva bounded forward! Ziva was born to pull; every muscle thrilled
to the surge, the tug, the stretch.

The Man praised Ziva, and she licked his hand eagerly.

Still, sometimes at night, when the wind carried the song of the wolves, Ziva wanted to run wild. She tore at the snow to get away, but the chain held her back.

Those mornings, the Man saw the mounded snow and understood. A day would come when Ziva would have to choose.

Would she stay . . . or go?

Now it was winter solstice in Alaska.

Daylight was short. The wind blew across the snow, whispering,
This is the day!

Ziva was new to a sled, so the Man paired her with a skookum
dog in front of the wheel dogs, where she would be close to him.

The team went crazy as the Man hitched them up.

They couldn't wait to run.

The dogs leaned into the wind, lapped the cold, and cocked
their ears back to hear the Man.
"*Gee!* . . . *Haw!* . . . *On-by!*" he called softly, and the dogs did it.

They moved as a team—the lead dog, two swing dogs, Ziva and the skookum dog, two wheel dogs, and the Man. The team ran till long shadows scraped the snow.

The sun set against their backs. Now it was stone-bone cold.

When it was time for si-wash, the Man built a fire and the dogs settled into the snow around it. The Man watched Ziva turn away from the fire and face the moon. And he knew . . .

The wind howled.

This is . . .

A wolf called.

This is . . .

Ziva called back . . .

This is the night!
She dug at the snow and threw her shoulders against the chain.
But there was no chain. There was nothing to hold her back.

Ziva tore into the night!
She ran and ran and ran as if she would never stop.
One hill, another, another, over the snow, over the ice.

Ziva had run a long way, and now she was hungry. When she spied a rabbit, her stomach roared like a hungry bear. The rabbit froze and twitched its ears. Ziva bounded after the rabbit. She was fast—but the rabbit was faster.

Now Ziva rested. The moon made dark shadows on the snow.
The wind cried between the pine trees. *Oooooo . . . ooooooo. . . .*
Ziva cocked her ears. Was it the wind or was it a wolf?
Ooooooo . . .
There, large against the moon—a wolf!

Ziva slunk toward the wolf. The wolf stepped forward.
Slowly, slowly, Ziva and the wolf approached, until at last
they stood together.

Cautiously, they sniffed each other.

The wolf smelled wild, like the wind. Ziva sniffed her own fur.
She smelled like the wind, too. But there was something else—
she also smelled like the Man! The Man's smell was her smell now.

Ziva's heart pulled. The Man! She missed the Man and his gentle hand. Ziva worked the trail for his praise. She shadowed his boot steps, she wanted to be close.

Ziva turned away from the wolf and ran. She ran and ran.

The Man heard her before he saw her. He squinted through the spinning snow . . . and there she was. Ziva!

Tears stung at the Man's eyes. So much did he love the wind-wild dog. So much did he want her to stay with him. He knelt in the snow and held out his hand to her.

Ziva paused, then ran toward him.

The Man patted her ruff and bear-hugged her. Ziva licked the Man's face, his ears, between the fingers of his hands.

Then she curled up and settled down beside him, pointing her nose into the wind.

Author's Notes

Alaska Alaska is our forty-ninth state and is sometimes called "Land of the Midnight Sun." That's because at the time of the summer solstice, June 21, the sun shines all day and all night. At the winter solstice, however, there are only a few hours of daylight.

Campfire First, a musher lays a "net" of spruce branches over the deep snow—otherwise the fire melts a hole in the snow and goes out. Then, the musher cuts down a thick spruce tree. He makes a fire out of kindling (small sticks) and the spruce tree. As the tree burns in half, he stacks the two pieces for a bigger fire. The musher warms up with the fire, but the dogs don't need to—they're warm enough!

Commands A musher gives his commands in a soft voice. His commands tell the team what to do, and include *hike*, *gee*, *haw*, *on-by*, and *whoa*.

Dog's ears A sled dog cocks its ears toward the musher when they're racing. A musher can often tell what a dog is thinking and feeling by the way its ears are bent. When the dog's ears cock forward, there may be something on the trail that the musher can't see.

Dog's eyes A sled dog's eyes are rimmed in black, which protects them from the glare of the sun on snow. Some dogs have brown eyes, and some have blue. A few huskies, like Ziva, have one brown eye and one blue. Blue eyes are reflected red by firelight, and brown eyes are reflected green.

Gee Command meaning "turn right."

Haw Command meaning "turn left."

Hike Command meaning "let's go."

Huskies These dogs are specially bred to pull a sled in very cold weather. Huskies' fur is so thick that they become hot when it's warmer than zero degrees Fahrenheit.

Lead dog This is a position of honor and is earned with time, faithfulness, intelligence, and courage. A new dog like Ziva could never be a lead, because she has to earn the team's trust.

Musher Man or woman who trains and drives a sled-dog team.

Si-wash A rest stop.

On-by Command meaning "go straight."

Skookum dog This term comes from gold rush days and means "a wise old dog." When a musher is introducing a new dog to his team, he'll pair it with a skookum dog who will help the new dog along its way.

Swing dogs Dogs behind the lead.

Wheel dogs Dogs closest to the sled. These dogs have to be quick enough to stay out of the way of the sled. They're often the strongest dogs, too.

Whoa Command meaning "stop."

Winter solstice The winter solstice, the shortest day of the year, usually falls on December 21. Many places in Alaska have just four or five hours of sunlight then. The sun is very low but very bright. Several hours of darkness follow the sun, before the moon lights the sky. Those dark hours are the coldest for a musher, who looks forward to the "heat" of the moon. The moon, of course, gives off no heat, but as one musher says, "When you're that cold, you take what you can get."

Working a dog A good dog man puts a harness on a dog first, until the dog is comfortable with it. Then the musher adds a branch to the back, so the dog gets used to the bump of something behind it. After that, the new dog is introduced to the team. He will be paired with a skookum dog and put in front of the wheel dogs until the newcomer gains confidence.